FUELING WOMEN TO CHANGE THE WORLD

By

JASMINE SMART

TABLE OF CONTENT

DEDICATION

This book is dedicated to God almighty the author and finisher of our faith, who gave me the wisdom, understanding,inspiration and the enablement through writing this book

ACKNOWLEDGEMENTS

I sincerely appreciate God almighty, the giver of life, for his grace, mercy, love and inspiration granted to me for the foundation of wisdom and knowledge for his kindness which endures forever to him be all the glory and honor This project is dedicated to God almighty the author and finisher of our faith, who gave me the wisdom, understanding and the enablement through this work

My profound gratitude goes to my colleague miss fortune who was with me all through this work may God bless you

Chapter 1

INTRODUCTION

The planet earth has over seven billion people as its inhabitants with almost half of this number as females. Change-makers, as they can be called, is an integral part of the society and are popularly referred to as the 'the gentle storm'. they are an important target group whose contributions to the development of the society have been applauded. This coupled with other reasons facilitated their inclusion in the sustainable development goals 2030. The reasons to focus on girl's issues are compelling as they develop into women who are the sole determinant of the potency of the generations being birthed. Much attention must be showered on girls especially as the number of females involved in the delinquency in society continues to grow. Girls of various communities of the world have different living conditions, some having to develop and grow under ideal conditions while others experience poor care, degradation, pain, and reproach. This is unfair as every girl child is entitled to a care filled life and authentic development. For too long, underprivileged girls have been punished for being victims, for not being boys, and being misunderstood because girls' development does not mirror that of boys.

Young girls worldwide are subjected to endure and suffer challenges such as gender-based violence, lack of education, gender discrimination, victimization by social vices, early/forced marriage, search for identity, social and parental pressure, poor access to healthcare, drug/substance abuse, malnutrition/poor food intake, communication, bad parenting, life skills (communication, decision making, goal setting) low self-esteem, fear of failure, poor hygiene amongst others. All these pose a threat to her quality of life preventing the girl child from reaching her full potential.

Like female juvenile delinquents, women who commit crimes have been an invisible minority whose needs, histories, and issues have gone largely undocumented (Belknap, 1996). A recent increase in the female crime rate is drawing more attention to this population, just as increases in arrests of juvenile females are drawing attention to young female offenders.

Although research on the causes of criminal behaviour in women remains scarce, many women currently serving sentences report that they can see a link between their adult offense and their history of sexual victimization, drug abuse, and prostitution (Belknap, 1996). For many of the women currently housed in prisons, these issues have gone unaddressed and untreated since childhood.

The combination of these factors makes the timing appropriate to focus specifically on the needs of the girls of today, who will become the women of tomorrow. This encourages empowering young women to defend themselves, assert their rights, overcome abuse, aspire to rewarding and lucrative careers, and lead healthy, independent lives. Efforts to address these issues led to the adoption of various strategies towards making girls relevant in every sphere of life in society.

CHAPTER 2

REASON WHY A GIRL CHILD SHOULD BE EMPOWERED

1. It's her right.

Fundamentally, this is a human rights issue. Discrimination has no place in the 21st century, and every girl has the right to go to school, stay safe from violence, access health services, and fully participate in her community.

2. Empowered girls mean healthier families.

When girls are educated, healthy, and empowered, families are healthier. According to UNESCO, 2.1 million children under age 5 were saved between 1990 and 2009 because of improvements in girls' education. And closing the gap in the unmet need for family planning for the 225 million girls and women who want to delay or avoid pregnancy but aren't using modern contraception would reduce maternal deaths by 67% and newborn deaths by 77%.

 3. Empowered girls are key to breaking the cycle of poverty for families around the world.

Research from the Brookings Institution has found that every additional year of school increases a girls' eventual wages by an average of 12% – earnings she invests back into her family. Empowered, educated girls have healthier, better educated children and higher wages – helping to break the cycle of poverty.

4. Empowered girls strengthen economies.

According to a new Brookings report, "Increasing the number of women completing secondary education by just 1 percent could increase a country's economic growth by 0.3 percent." Additionally, a report just released by the McKinsey Global Institute found that if women's level of participation in the labor market was the same as men's it would add up to $28 trillion to annual global GDP in 2025.

5. Did we mention it's the right thing to do?

Investing in girls is one of the smartest things we can do to promote a healthier, more prosperous world. More importantly, it's the right thing to do. Every girl has the right to be in charge of her future and her fate, and we have the collective obligation to protect her rights and promote her wellbeing.

This is a key priority for the UN. To join our movement to support UN programs that empower adolescent girls

CHAPTER 3

WHY EMPOWER GIRLS

The empowerment of girls is one of the most important concerns of the 21st century. In the 1970s when women empowerment was first invoked by the Third World feminist and women organizations, it was inexplicably used to frame and facilitate the struggle for social justice and women equality through a transformation of economic, social and political structures at national and international levels (Bisnath & Elson, 2003). The need to empower women seems to center on the fact that women have the potentials to contribute to the development process but are constrained by some factors that render them powerless. While the reasons for any particular woman's powerlessness are many and vary, it may be necessary to consider what women have in common in this respect.

Empowerment, therefore, requires an analysis of women's subordination, the formulation of an alternative more satisfactory set of arrangements to those which exist. These can be achieved through the alleviation of the burden of domestic labour and childcare, the removal of institutionalized forms of discrimination, the establishment of political equality, improving the economic status of women, freedom of choice over childbearing, and taking measures against male violence and control over women (Molyneaux, 1985). In other words, empowerment requires the transformation of structures of subordination through changes in the law, property rights, and other institutions that reinforce and perpetuate male domination (Batliwala, 1994). This could be done by improving the educational, political and economic status of women to enable them to participate actively in development processes.

If 50% of the global population suffers daily discrimination, increased risk of assault, and all kinds of other horrid problems just by being female, we can say that empowerment should be a top priority. The term empowerment originates from American community psychology and is associated with the social scientist Julian Rappaport (1981). Girl empowerment is essentially the upliftment of economic, social status of traditionally underprivileged girls in society. It involves the building up of a society where girls can breathe without the fear of oppression, exploitation, apprehension, discrimination, and feeling of persecution which goes with being a woman in a traditionally male-dominated structure. Empowerment is a multidimensional social process that helps people gain control over their lives. It is a process to foster power in people for use in their own lives, their community, and society at large.

The continued persistence of girl's problems in the areas of gender equality, gender roles, improved social status, etc., raises several questions about the empowerment strategies of governmental and non-governmental agencies. Are the strategies based on faulty theoretical assumptions? Is their application in the situation faulty? What is the problem of their application in the Nigerian context?

Fundamentally, this is a human rights issue. Discrimination has no place in the 21st century, and every girl has the right to go to school, stay safe from violence, access health services, and fully participate socially in her community. Secondly empowered girls mean healthier families. When girls are educated, healthy, and empowered, families, are healthier. According to UNESCO, 2.1 million children under age 5 were saved between 1990 and 2009 because of improvements in girls' education. And closing the gap in the unmet need for family planning for the 225 million girls and women who want to delay or avoid pregnancy but aren't using modern contraception would reduce maternal deaths by 67% and newborn deaths by 77%.

Also, empowered girls are keys to breaking the cycle of poverty for families around the world.

Research has found that every additional year of school increases a girls' eventual wages by an average of 12% – earnings she invests back into her family. Empowered, educated girls have healthier, better-educated children and higher wages –helping to break the cycle of poverty.

1:Empowered girls strengthen economies.

According to a new Brookings report, "Increasing the number of women completing secondary education by just 1 percent could increase a country's economic growth by 0.3 percent." Additionally, a report just released by the McKinsey Global Institute found that if women's level of participation in the labour market was the same as men's it would add up to $28 trillion to annual global GDP in 2025. Financial empowerment of women spurs economic growth within a country...which can lead to the country becoming more stable, reducing poverty, and becoming a bigger player in the global market. Having more bargaining chips on the table can help a country's leaders make better deals with other governing bodies, as well as receive aid and support more effectively. Bottom line: More empowered women mean more safety and security

2: Better lives for men

If women are empowered, that frees men from the pressure to be the primary wage-earner and shows little boys they can explore all aspects of who they are, without paying attention to roles that are traditionally "masculine" or "feminine." Men will have more freedom to work part-time or take care of children, which frees them up for other more interesting activities. What's the advantage of this? Society loosens up, and everyone is free to be who they truly want to be.

3:Better literature!

Two-thirds of the 774 million adult illiterates across the world are women. Imagine if the best book you've ever read was going to be written by a woman who hasn't yet been taught to read? Women's empowerment will lead to more journalism, better books and movies, and more interesting stories being told. As a kid who grew up with my nose in a book, this sounds like the best possible outcome for everyone

4:More incredible inventions

Women have been innovating and excelling in the fields of science and math for hundreds of years...despite facing harassment and discrimination, empowering girls means more women in STEM (Science, Technology, Engineering, and Mathematics). Many empowered girls have made life-saving inventions for example pee-powered generator built by a group of 14-year-old girls in Nigeria and a Turkish girl who figured out how to turn banana to bioplastic. Another example is Ada Lovelace who invented the first computer program.More empowered girls then would automatically lead to more incredible inventions.

Empowerment of girls results in saving the planet!

If fertility rates continue the way they are now, scientists estimate the world's population will swell to 10 billion by 2081. That's 10 billion people competing for food, water, and other resources. One of the best ways to ensure that we live in a safe, healthy, and sustainable world is to support women who want reproductive healthcare and effective contraception. Nobody wants to worry about fighting for freshwater, and empowering women with voluntary family planning is a sure-fire route to a happier, healthier planet.

We will see more and better food for everyone

The vast majority (80%) of agricultural workers in the world are female. Empowerment to grow, buy, and sell the crops they want decreases undernourishment in producing countries and increases the amount of food available for export. Did you eat today? Thank a (female) farmer.

Political empowerment means more and better policies

When policymakers are mostly men, it seems like the needs of women (and a lot of other people) get thrown by the wayside. When women stand up in political forums, we get legislation that can save lives, protect young girls, and provide access to needed healthcare. If we want our daughters to have the care they need in the future, we need more women in political power now. Empowerment for everyone!

Overturn nasty beauty standards that contribute to low self-esteem

Everyone's seen beauty magazines, with their focus on hairless, sculpted, unreal, bleached and plucked specimens of humanity...and that's just the men. The current beauty standards teach everybody to hate them because they're too fat, too hairy, too old, or just plain not airbrushed enough. If we're willing to empower women to accept who they are and how they look (beautiful!), men will reap the benefits and stop having to worry about their appearances and feel bad too. Throw the beauty magazines away before we all feel ugly.

CHAPTER 4

HOW DO WE EMPOWER GIRLS?

developing and adopting policies to prohibit gender bias in placement and treatment of young offenders," and for "establishing programs to ensure that female youth have access to the full range of health and mental health services, treatment for physical or sexual assault and abuse, self-defense instruction, education in parenting, education in general, and other training and vocational services." (Juvenile Justice and Delinquency Prevention Act, 1992)

1:EDUCATION

Education is a potent and indispensable tool in the emancipation and empowerment of girls. The greatest single factor which can incredibly improve the status of females in any society is education. It is indispensable that it enables them not only to gain more knowledge about the world but helps her to get status, positive self-esteem and self-confidence, necessary courage and inner strength to face challenges in life. It also facilitates the procurement of a job and supplements the income of the family and improves social status. Educated girls can play an equal role as boys in nation-building. Therefore, there is no denying the fact that education empowers girls. Literacy skills (reading and writing) would enable women to have a broader picture of the world at large.

2:SAFE SPACE

A safe space is a place where girls of same age group meet to discuss issues regarding their life. A safe space curriculum is structured in such a way that topics cover almost all aspects of a girl's life. Create a safe space to talk about issues like reproductive health, gender equity and rights of women. Safe spaces would also enable them to be able to talk about the problems they face as girls, boost their self-esteem, confidence and helping them to be more comfortable about sharing their opinions. It also would help them acquire life skills (communication, decision making, and goal setting).

3:JOB SKILLS AND SEED BUSINESSES

A girl can be empowered by giving her support for economic independence and mobility through vocational and entrepreneurial training thereby increasing savings and income.

4:ACCESS TO HEALTH SERVICES

Youth-friendly/healthcare services where girls can get counseling and medical help without the fear of being judged by anybody. Girls usually need an adult to

5:BUILD NETWORKS

Girls that have been empowered would support greater opportunities to effect change in their respective communities. They can meet to create a network of activities targeted to reach other underprivileged girls to enable them also reach their full potential

6:CREATE PUBLIC LEADERS

Girls can also be empowered by training them on leadership. This would enable them to develop a sense of responsibility and belonging and can spur political interest in them.

21 Strengths of Women That Should be Celebrated More

9 months ago

CHAPTER 5

21 Strengths of Women That Should be Celebrated More

Today women are making strides and breaking barriers. It is not uncommon to see women excelling in traditionally male-dominated fields such as politics, finance, and sports.

But there's so much more than that... women have many strengths that should be celebrated! In this blog post, we will explore 21 of these qualities—from kindness to perseverance—that make women both strong and beautiful.

1. Women are great listeners

Women are great listeners women tend to excel at communication, especially when it comes to building rapport with other women. Women have the ability to not only listen carefully but also empathize and respond in a way that makes others feel understood.

2. Women have a lot of love to give

This is apparent in the way they treat others. Women have been shown to be more compassionate, considerate, and generous than men when it comes to dealing with other people.

3. Women are brave

Women have a lot of bravery and courage that is oftentimes underappreciated. Research has shown that women tend to be more risk-averse than men when it comes to financing, loans, etc., but they also take greater risks in other areas such as career changes and relocating for the sake of their family.

5. Women are hard workers

Women have a great work ethic and they tend to be highly motivated. Women view career advancement as being important, which is why women also earn higher degrees at much higher rates than men do.

6. Women are problem-solvers

Women have a special talent for being able to solve problems. Whether it's at work, within their family, or in the community women tend to be really good about working through different scenarios and coming up with solutions.

women strengths

7. Women are good communicators

Women tend to be really good at communicating, both verbally and non-verbally. Women have a way of expressing themselves that is oftentimes more effective than the ways in which men communicate.

8. Women are empathetic

Women have a special talent for being able to empathize with others. Women tend to be more understanding of the experiences women face on a daily basis and they can sympathize with other women in ways that men simply cannot, which is why women make great mentors.

9. Women are very resilient

Women have a lot of resilience that is oftentimes thrown into question. Women tend to be really good at overcoming challenges and they're not afraid to persevere through tough times in order to achieve their goals.

10. Women are creative

Women have a special talent for being able to be creative and come up with new ideas. Women tend to excel in the arts as well as STEM fields which women bring valuable skills such as collaboration, brainstorming, and problem-solving into these industries.

11. Women are great multi-taskers

One of women's most useful talents is their ability to multitask. Women can juggle many things at one time and women tend to be really good about managing multiple responsibilities throughout the day such as family, work, social life, etc.

12. Women are compassionate

Women have a lot of compassion that they show towards others women feel empathy for those who are less fortunate and women also tend to be the first ones to offer help when it's needed.

13. Women are great team players

Women love being part of a community, whether that means within their family or at work women enjoy helping others succeed as well as working together with other people in order to meet group goals. This is why women tend to build great teams.

14. Women are strong

Women have a lot of strength that they show on a daily basis proves they can handle difficult situations, criticism, and different types of stress in ways that most men simply cannot women persevere through the toughest times because women know how important it is to continue fighting for what you believe in.

15. Women are great listeners

Women have a special talent for being able to listen and women tend to be better at listening than men do women focus on what other people say and they pay attention which makes women great conversationalists.

16. Women strive for success

One of the strengths that women possess is their desire to advance in their careers women see the value in being dedicated to their work so women are more likely than men are to put in extra hours at work women genuinely enjoy working hard because women know that having a career is one of the best ways for women to become independent and self-sufficient.

17. Women have high emotional intelligence

Women tend to be really good at understanding women's feelings and emotions women have a special talent for being able to identify other people's feelings, as well as their own women, can easily articulate how they feel about certain situations which makes women good at expressing themselves.

18. Women never stop learning

Women know that they can always continue growing as people, so women strive to become better every day women actively look for ways to learn new things women always have a desire to improve themselves which makes women lifelong learners.

19. Women have a strong sense of intuition

Women have a special talent for being able to make women feel safe women are great at reading people's intentions and women trust their instincts which makes women good judges of character.

20. Women see the silver lining in life

One of womens' greatest strengths is their optimism women tend to be really good at looking on the bright side, even in the worst of situations women have a strong tendency to see the positive in every situation which means women are more likely than men to be hopeful about their futures.

21. Women are great leaders

Women tend to be great at leading others women have the skills necessary for taking charge and making decisions women also show strength by being able to take criticism, so women can handle constructive feedback better than men do.

Economically empowered women foster a sense of identity.

French champagne, Argentinian beef, and Belgian chocolate – these fine products are intimately associated with their countries of origin and serve as sources of national pride. In Moldova, a country that gained independence only a generation ago and still struggles with its place in a complexgeopolitical environmental citizen   are striving to develop locally-made products that could reach similar renown and serve as points of collective pride empowering NG   women-led and women-founded enterprises in the apparel sector has helped Moldova take a step in that direction. Joining together under the brand Din Inima: Branduri de Moldova (From the Heart: Brands of Moldova), women entrepreneurs have taken Moldovan-made apparel from a low-cost and low-quality necessity into a runway-worthy product, visibly increasing consumer loyalty and pride in locally-made apparel. Clothing will, of course, not single-handedly strengthen national identity, but the apparel sector's success has helped foster a sense of national pride and cohesion. Aspiring entrepreneurs and artisans now have a model to draw from as they seek to make a name for Moldovan products globally.

Economically empowered women, with a strong sense of community, can also be an important piece of the puzzle to countering violent extremism. In a place like the Pankisi Gorge area of Georgia, inhabited largely by minority ethnic groups, creating economic opportunity for women allows them to pass on values of inter-ethnic trust and community identity to their children, laying the foundation for the development of a more resilient and stable community.

Economically empowered women serve as climate-change-adaptation champions.Adapting to climate change requires a willingness to do things differently than they have been done before and an ability to forego short-term gains in favor of long-term ones. In Morocco, women entrepreneurs have demonstrated these traits, recognizing success in their ventures and serving as climate change champions. When soil degradation and water scarcity made it increasingly difficult to make a living in Moroccan agricultural communities, Moroccan women spearheaded shifts in agricultural practices. Women producers switched from growing water-intensive traditional crops to less water-intensive medicinal and aromatic plants; they also began using renewable energy sources. The women are now securing a more sustainable income stream for their family products. further desertification through more efficient use of resources. Their entrepreneurial ability to adapt has allowed these women to help their families and help the planet.

Economically empowered women shift gender norms.It's human nature: the first time we see something we deem odd, we stop, stare, and gossip about it to our neighbors. The second time we see it, we shake our head and sigh. The third time, we simply shrug our shoulders and move on; what was once odd has become normal. In Bangladesh's staunchly patriarchal society, historically, women have been discouraged from working outside of the home. But, women pioneers in the dairy sector are now taking on roles such as mobile input providers and artificial inseminators, which is contributing to a shift in gender norms. Women working in these positions have improved daily milk production, increased household incomes, earned women respect for their technical competence, and begun normalizing women's work outside the home.

Economically empowered women contribute to better health and nutrition outcomes.Increasing women's incomes improves food security for children, by increasing the quantity, diversity, and nutrition value of food consumed in households. The same principle applies for women's and children's health; in numerous development contexts, a woman will have a hard time taking a day off and travelling to a distant clinic for services while her overwhelming concern remains how to feed her children. When a woman's livelihood becomes stable because she learns to grow a more profitable crop or obtains financing to expand her business from a local village savings and lending association, she is able to afford more diverse, nutritious foods and take time off of work to seek health care for herself and for her family.

This week, as we continue to explore the meaning of economic empowerment, I am reminded of a woman who grows flowers in western Georgia. Combining her horticultural skills with business acumen, she ingeniously leveraged existing transportation networks, societal trust, and established relationships to grow her business, including using the ubiquitous marshrutka (public minibus) network to distribute fresh flowers around the region. Her bravery and ingenuity, and the bravery and ingenuity of all other women entrepreneurs, are an inspiration. Much progress remains to be made in the years to come, but it's certain that supporting women such as these in their endeavors is not only the right thing to do – it's the smart thing to do.

It's not always easy being a woman in the world, but you should take pride in your strengths. Showing love for these qualities can help us celebrate each other more and find solidarity with women who are struggling to be themselves.

The 21 Strengths of Women That Should Be Celebrated More is an article that highlights some of the best parts about being female that we often overlook or forget to mention when talking about gender roles.

These traits are worth celebrating! Check out this list if you're feeling lost today because it will remind you how strong and amazing women truly are. Which one of these attributes resonates most strongly with you?

Strengths for Decision Making and Judgment

A leader is able to make quick decisions and stick by them. Here are some examples of strengths as they relate to sound judgment:

Gathers important information

Makes decisions regarding the best action to take

Implements the course of action

Communicates and explains decisions

Follows up on progress of actions

Learns from previous mistakes

Organizing and Planning Strengths

Of course, organization is key when running a large team. Here are key strengths as they relate to organization and planning:

Defines concrete goals

Explains goals in detail

Creates a plan to achieve goals

Gathers and assigns resources

Motivates the staff to achieve the highest level of performance

Evaluates progress and provides feedback

Problem Solving Strengths

Similar to an ability to make quick decisions, sound problem-solving skills are integral in a team leader. Here are some examples of problem-solving strengths:

Recognizes the problem

Analyzes relevant information

Understands cause and effect relationships

Develops possible solutions

Chooses the best solution and implements it

Personal and Professional Strength-Building

CHAPTER 6

Women key to success

The key to succeeding in various situations, personal or professional, is to identify your strengths and ensure they fit the situation or task you're undertaking. Focus on what you're good at rather than what you're capable of. Then, you'll then be more engaged in the task and able5 ways to find out what your strengths are

One of the best ways to help you decide what kinds of jobs might suit you is to ask yourself, and those around you, some questions related to who you are, your strengths and interests. Also think about what jobs are in demand and expected to continue growing. Sound good? Here are 5 tips to get you started:

1. Ask around

A great way to find out more Urself is to ask people you like, trust and respect what they think you're best at. Why not make a list of people you can ask about the kinds of jobs they think might suit your strengths and personality, and why? They could be members of your family, a teacher or lecturer or somebody else you're close to. If you're not sure how or what to ask about, here are some ideas to get you started.

2. Discover your personality

Check out the module, 'Discover your personality' for tips on how to get a better understanding of what makes you tick. Thinking about your personality is a great way to start identifying the kind of jobs which could be a good match.

3. Write down what you do

Over the course of a week, think about the 5 things you most enjoy doing and write them down. Challenge yourself to really think about why it is you like them. For example:

I have a blog that I update regularly with opinions, short stories and other bits and pieces I find around the web. I set aside time in the week to write and find stuff to publish, then I schedule posts on social media that link to my site.

In this instance, it's clear that this person likes being organised, staying up to date with popular culture, and works well alone. Thinking about the kinds of activities you enjoy, or naturally find yourself doing, is a great way to help identify your strengths and skills.

4. Look for patterns

Once you have answers from a few different places, highlight any areas that come up frequently, or character traits that lots of people have identified. Try asking yourself the same questions and compare the answers to see if you agree. The skills which come up most frequently will most likely be your strongest. Now you can use the Wheel of Strengths to match these up with potential careers.

5. Keep an open mind

Some of the answers and results you get might be surprising, or highlight aspects of your personality that you hadn't considered. Don't dismiss these. 2The idea is to get a better picture of yourself, and that includes the image you present to other people, as well as what you're good at and things that you could improve. These unexpected qualities might lend themselves to an area of work that you had never considered before.

Look at the required skills section on some job adverts and compare which ones you have. You will always be growing your skills so don't worry if you don't get complete matches. For more tips and guidance on developing .

CHAPTER 7

THE GLOBAL ROLE OF WOMEN – CARETAKERS, CONSCIENCE, FARMERS, EDUCATORS AND ENTREPRENEURS

Role of women Africa

Throughout history, the central role of women in society has ensured the stability, progress and long-term development of nations. Globally, women comprise 43 percent of the world's agricultural labor force – rising to 70 percent in some countries. For instance, across Africa, 80 percent of the agricultural production comes from small farmers, most of whom are rural women. It's widely accepted that agriculture can be the engine of growth and poverty reduction in developing nations. Women, notably mothers, play the largest role in decision-making about family meal planning and diet. And, women self-report more often their initiative in preserving child health and nutrition.

The Role of Women as Caretakers

Women are the primary caretakers of children and elders in every country of the world. International studies demonstrate that when the economy and political organization of a society change, women take the lead in helping the family adjust to new realities and challenges. They are likely to be the prime initiator of outside assistance, and play an important role in facilitating (or hindering) changes in family life.

"Rural women play a key role in supporting their households and communities in achieving food and nutrition security, generating income, and improving rural livelihoods and overall well-being."

The Role of Women as Educators

The contribution of women to a society's transition from pre-literate to literate likewise is undeniable. Basic education is key to a nation's ability to develop and achieve sustainability targets. Research has shown that education can improve agricultural productivity, enhance the status of girls and women, reduce population growth rates, enhance environmental protection, and widely raise the standard of living.

It is the mother in the family who most often urges children of both genders to attend – and stay – in school. The role of women is at the front end of the chain of improvements leading to the family's, the community's long-term capacity.

The Role of Women in the Workforce

Today, the median female share of the global workforce is 45.4 percent. Women's formal and informal labor can transform a community from a relatively autonomous society to a participant in the national economy. Despite significant obstacles, women's small businesses in rural developing communities not only can be an extended family's lifeline, but can form a networked economic foundation for future generations. The role of women in the urban and rural workforce has expanded exponentially in recent decades.

The theme for International Women's Day 2019 "Think equal, build smart, innovate for change," was chosen to identify innovative ways to advance gender equality and the empowerment of women, accelerating the 2030 Agenda, building momentum for the effective implementation of the new U.N. Sustainable Development Goals. Of course, women's opportunities still lag behind those of men worldwide. But, the historic and current role of women is indisputable. "When women are empowered and can claim their rights and access to land, leadership, opportunities and choices, economies grow, food security is enhanced and prospects are improved for current and future generations."

Role of a woman in a home

1. As a wife:

Woman is man's helpmate, partner and comrade. She sacrifices her personal pleasure and ambitions, sets standard of morality, relieves stress and strain, tension of husband, maintains peace and order in the household. Thereby she creates necessary environment for her male partner to think mqore about the economic upliftment of family. She is the source of inspiration to man for high endeavour and worth achievements in life.

She stands by him in all the crises as well as she shares with him all successes and attainments. She is the person to whom he turns for love, sympathy, understanding, comfort and recognition. She is the symbol of purity, faithfulness and submission and devotion to her husband.

2. As an Administrator and Leader of the Household:

A well-ordered disciplined household is essential to normal family life. The woman in the family assumes this function. She is the chief executive of an enterprise. She assigns duties among family members according to their interest and abilities and provides resources in-term of equipment and materials to accomplish the job.

She plays a key role in the preparation and serving of meals, selection and care of clothing, laundering, furnishing and maintenance of the house. As an administrator, she organizes various social functions in the family for social development. She also acts as a director of recreation. She plans various recreational activities to meet the needs of young and old members of the family.

3. As a Manager of Family Income:

Woman acts as the humble manager of the family income. It is her responsibility to secure maximum return from every pye spent. She always prefers to prepare a surplus budget instead of a deficit budget. She is very calculating loss and gain while spending money. She distributes judiciously the income on different heads such as necessities, comforts and luxuries. The woman in the family also contributes to the family income through her own earning within or outside the home. She has positive contribution to the family income by the work.

She herself performs in the home and uses waste products for productive purposes.

4. As a Mother:

The whole burden of child bearing and greater part of child rearing task are carried out by the woman in the family. She is primarily responsible for the child's habit of self-control, orderliness, industriousness, theft or honesty. Her contacts with the child during the most formative period of his development sets up his behaviour pattern. She is thus responsible for the maintenance of utmost discipline in the family.

She is the first teacher of the child. She transmits social heritage to the child. It is from mother that the child learns the laws of the race, the manner of men, moral code and ideals. The mother, because of her intimate and sustained contact with the child, she is able to discover and nurture child's special traits aptitudes and attitudes which subsequently play a key role in the shaping of his personality.

As a mother she is the family health officer. She is very much concerned about the physical wellbeing of every member of the family, the helpless infant, the sickly child, the adolescent youth, senescent parent. She organizes the home and its activities in such a way so that each member of the family has proper food, adequate sleep and sufficient recreation. She made the home a place of quite comfortable and appropriate setting for the children through her talent. Besides, she cultivates taste in interior design and arrangement, so that the home becomes an inviting, restful and cheerful place.

The mother is the central personality of the home and the family circle. All the members turn to her for sympathy, understanding and recognition. Woman devotes her time, labour and thought for the welfare of the members of the family. For the unity of interacting personalities, man provides the temple woman provides the ceremonies and the atmosphere.

The woman performs the role of wife, partner, organizer, administrator, director, re-creator, disburser, economist, mother, disciplinarian, teacher, health officer, artist and queen in the family at the same time. Apart from it, woman plays a key role in the socio-economic development of the society.

Modern education and modern economic life use to compel woman more and more to leave the narrow sphere of the family circle and work side by side for the enrichment of society. She can be member of any women's organisation and can launch various programmes like literacy programme such as adult education, education for disadvantaged girls etc.

The purpose of introducing such literacy programme is to raise the society as education enables women to respond to opportunities, to challenge their traditional roles and to change their life circumstances. Education is the most important instrument for human resource development.

Women are the key to sustainable development and quality of life. So they should be members of community centre or club to disseminate knowledge about handicraft, cottage industries, food preservation and low cost nutritious diet to people belonging low socio economic status for their economic upliftment. They should act as leaders of the society to raise voice against women violence, exploitation in household as well as in work place, dowry prohibition superstition and other social atrocities.

For many people, finding a good wife is a blind man's buff because they don't know the qualities of a good wife to search for. It is important to mention that knowing the qualities of a good wife will guide your search when you are ready to get one.

CHAPTER 8

Women as role model

It's important now more than ever for women to support each other. Utilizing the power of community is truly the catalyst that will evoke change and equality, helping women flourish in our careers and personal development. It is through these bonds that we learn to appreciate and become inspired by the stories shared of the women we call #FemaleRoleModel.

There are many qualities used to determine Female Role Model and everyone's definition looks different. At Ellevate, there are many qualities that we value and strive to emulate. The women we admire are a diverse group who share some of our core values and work to create unity and equality. Our female role models take "women supporting women" very seriously. Lifting women up and encouraging each other to reach their fullest potential is the only way we can make change. Reaching out to women can make a huge difference, and the women we admire are constantly lifting others up.

A female role model does not have to be a celebrity. She is ANY woman you look up to. She is a woman who makes a difference, whether it is in the little things she does in her everyday life or the grand gestures made in the public eye. Being a female role model requires a confidence not rooted solely in career or status, but in seeing the value in herself. This quality is exactly why female role models are so important, and at Ellevate we're committed to celebrating it.

Since we are still working to close the gender gap, it's important for younger generations and those who aspire to great things to see the women they look up to in prominent roles. Having positive images of powerful, intelligent women making change in the world sends the message that your opportunities are limitless, regardless of your gender. This attention to female role models will bring about some great leaders (and positive change) for years to come. It's about time we give women the credit they deserve.

Last year, we looked at some of our female role models and how they make a huge difference for women everywhere. This year we're taking another look at some more fierce women who inspire us every day, are rewriting history, and are paving the way for the next generation.

Women & the Community

Creating a space for women's voices to be heard is key since historically they have been overlooked and silenced (see Rosalind Franklin, The US Presidents, Shirley Chisholm, Amelia Earhart, any history book).

Women oftentimes have to work much harder than their male counterparts just to be heard. Because of this, being a community leader takes incredible determination and resilience.

Elizabeth Warren, the first female senator of Massachusetts, has been making waves in the media. Her strong beliefs in affordable and accessible education as well as gender equality have led her to be the voice of the future. Senator Warren is a big proponent of bringing young people into the political conversation and fighting for legislation that often gets overlooked. Her dedication to the community and determination to make change gives us serious confidence that women's voices will be heard (see: "Nevertheless, she persisted").

Gretchen Carlson, former Miss America and TV commentator, chooses to speak out when society suggests we stay silent. As a woman in television, she's faced her fair share of criticism and sexism. When Gretchen spoke out against sexual harassment in the workplace, she made it easier for other women to do the same. It is women like her, who are brave when others try to silence her, that help others feel their voices deserve to be heard.

Authenticity

Part of being a female role model is being true to yourself. Being able to stay true to your values and what you believe in can inspire others around you. The female role models we applaud also use their platform to highlight others whose voices are often overlooked.

When we look at female role models, we've been looking at women who are well established in their careers, but actress Yara Shahidi is using her burgeoning career to speak up on women's rights. With her strong social media presence, Shahidi has been making headlines as she uses her platform to represent those young women who feel underrepresented. She speaks up about representation of women of color on TV and how important it is for girls to see themselves on the screen in a positive light.

Shahidi speaks candidly about her experiences as a mixed race actress in the industry. In a conversation with Teen Vogue, she discusses her hopes for the future roles for women of color. "I want to see somebody who looks like me as the doctor and the criminal and the successful businessperson and the woman barely making a living. I want to see the spectrum."

Diversity

Including diversity in the conversation is important in helping all women feel represented. Many times discussions of feminism can exclude some groups, but many women are working to bridge that gap.

Tina Tchen, Former Executive Director of The White House Council on Women and Girls, is a woman who fights for gender equality every day and strives to make the government reflect

the population. In an interview with Makers, Tchen said, "Our public officials should reflect the diversity in our country and when women are half of our population, to have

them not even close to half of our public officials is a problem." Her work and drive to bring diversity into the government has led her to be the Executive Director of the Council of on Women and Girls. She also recognizes that there is work to be done for the transgender community and wants to ensure safety for ALL women.

Seeing such a diverse group of powerful and revolutionary women is truly inspiring. It is easy for girls to look at the media and become discouraged when they do not see themselves represented. However, our female role models continue to show us that women are making tremendous strides in our society and are the catalysts for change. Celebrating these women is one of the ways we can appreciate female role models, but supporting women in our everyday lives is how we can take action. We cannot succeed alone, but with a support system and mentors to help, success is inevitable. At Ellevate, we believe developing this support is key in accomplishing our goals, gaining success and connecting with incredible female role models.

CHAPTER 9

How to Be a Role Model for Girls

Together we can encourage the next generation of female leaders. Girls often look to the women in their lives for cues about how to think and act. When we speak confidently, take risks, and own our accomplishments, we set positive examples for girls to follow. There are countless opportunities every day to help girls gain the confidence and skills they need to lean in and take the lead.

Special thanks to Rachel Simmons and the team at Girls Leadership for their expert insights on empowering girls.

1. Coach Girls to Speak Confidently

Girls can undermine themselves when they speak.

Many girls use phrases like "kind of" and "sort of" to weaken their statements. Some introduce opinions with disclaimers ("I'm not sure if this is right, but . . .") or use upspeak so their statements sound like questions ("Martin Luther King, Jr., was a civil rights leader?"). These verbal crutches hinder a girl's ability to share her ideas clearly and confidently—a habit that often carries over into adulthood.

To help girls find their voice:

Speak with confidence so girls hear what it sounds like. Avoid hedging your opinions with disclaimers or apologies. If you observe a girl falling into these same habits, explain how it undermines the point she's trying to make. Remind her it's not just what you say that matters, it's how you say it, too.

2. Teach Girls to Navigate Conflict

Girls are often taught to suppress their feelings in order to get along with others.2

As a result, they do not learn to speak openly and manage conflict. Fast-forward to adulthood: too often women avoid giving each other honest input to avoid being seen as unkind or fall into the trap of personalizing constructive input we receive. Because we shy away from giving and getting direct feedback, many women miss out on the input we need to be our best selves and advance in our careers more quickly.

To help girls, do this:

Model honest, direct communication for the girls in your life. When faced with a difficult situation, talk to the people involved—not about them—and share your true feelings. Encourage girls to speak their mind and avoid social shortcuts like texting and social media. Role-play difficult conversations together, and ask girls to reflect on what worked and what didn't. Explain that conflict is an inevitable part of relationships—it's the way we handle it that matters.

3. Encourage Girls to Own Their Success

When girls are confident in their abilities, they are more likely to take the lead.3

The problem is that girls are often underestimated by others—and underestimate themselves—which erodes their confidence. When girls are complimented on their achievements, they also tend to deflect praise or minimize their accomplishments,4 yet internalizing success is an important part of building self-confidence.

These same dynamics carry over into adulthood. Women often get less credit for successes and can be blamed more for failures.5 We also tend to underestimate our own abilities and attribute our success to external factors such as "getting lucky" or "help from others."6 Because we receive less credit and give ourselves less credit, we often feel less self-assured, and it curbs our appetite for taking on new challenges.

To help girls, do this:

Model owning your accomplishments for the girls in your life. Say "thank you" when you receive a compliment instead of deflecting it. When girls see that it is okay to own their success, they will feel more comfortable doing it themselves. Moreover, look for opportunities to celebrate girls' success and acknowledge their strengths, and push back if they fall into the trap of sidestepping praise.

4. Inspire Girls to Go for It

Because girls often struggle with confidence and fear making mistakes, they are less likely to take risks.

Some girls don't speak up in class unless they're 100 percent sure they have the right answer, while others shy away from trying new subjects or activities. This same reluctance also holds women back. Compared to our male counterparts, we can be less likely to take on high-profile projects or lobby for more senior positions. Women often wait to apply for a job until they meet 100% of the hiring criteria, while men apply when they meet just 60%.[8]

Model taking healthy risks. Talk about the times you've stepped out of your comfort zone, and explain how good it feels when you succeed and how much you learn when you don't. When you hear girls say they're "not ready" or "can't do it," gently push back and remind them it's an opportunity to learn and grow. Make sure girls know that being brave is rarely about dramatic moments: it's a skill acquired, little by little, over time.

5. Celebrate Female Leadership

Girls and boys get very different messages about leadership.

We expect boys to lead, so we applaud them when they do. On the other hand, we expect girls to be kind and communal, so when they speak their mind or take the lead, they often face pushback. As a result, girls often worry they'll make people mad or be laughed at if they assume a leadership position.9 It's no wonder that by middle school, girls are less interested in leading than boys—a trend that continues into adulthood.10

Talk openly about your own experiences taking the lead and celebrate female leaders in your life and in the news. If you hear a girl being criticized for asserting herself or referred to as "bossy" or "aggressive," step in and explain she should be applauded, not chided, for her leadership skills. Finally, make sure girls understand the benefits of being a leader, like having a voice and making things happen!

The Power of Role Models in a girl's life

Girls are exposed to both positive and negative role models every day: a strong mother who stands up against domestic abuse or a female celebrity that uses her sex appeal to be popular. All of these people affect how a girl views her own potential. These are the people who girls use as references for whom they will become and whose behaviour they will emulate.

A girl needs to see confidence, leadership and accomplishment in other women in order to

envision herself with those qualities. A programme designed to empower girls must provide powerful, positive role models. As programme directors, it is helpful to expose girls to a diverse set of role models as consistently as possible. Strong role models can be women who are older, skilled athletes, coaches, community leaders, successful business people, celebrities, politicians, religious leaders, confident peers or any strong woman whose presence will resonate with the girls. Although there is power to showing girls women who are international heroines, there is also a power to exposing them to local people.

Local examples provide more easily imaginable visions of success. A key component to presenting girls with role models is to make sure the success experienced by the role models is attainable and replicable in their minds. Research has shown that when individuals feel that the role model in front of them has attained a status unreachable to them, their presence can actually be demoralizing.[1] If possible, find role models who exemplify an area in which girls have an interest and where they need help in personal development. Find a person who can share their personal experience with personal growth in that area. Men can certainly serve aspositive role models; however, there is an inherent value in same-gender role modelling.

Organize events where role models speak to girls about their experiences.

CHAPTER 10

REASON WHY WOMEN NEED A STRONG AND SUCCESSFUL ROLE MODELS

1:Try to pair up individual girls with older mentors with the intention of creating long-lasting relationships.

Take girls to see athletic events with older participants. Arrange a meet-and-greet afterwards to allow girls to interact with players.

Set up guest coaching sessions with successful coaches from your region.

Ensure that all those in positions of power within the organisation are serving as positive role models for participants.

Seek role models outside of the sport arena. Invite a successful businesswoman or female politician to come to the programme and speak to the girls.

Consider inviting men or women with a disability to come speak, as they often have a powerful impact on girls with and without disabilities.

Discuss the concept of "negative role modelling" with girls, i.e., simply because a person is successful does not mean that they are worthy of being a role model.

Challenge girls to evaluate virtues, values and expectations related to these role models.

. So that they can truly get the most out of their childhood!

Little girls need to know that it's okay to be a little girl. There is such a push to grow up too soon. But strong role models remind us that each stage of our lives is to be celebrated and lived out fully. So, let your daughter be a kid to the fullest. Remind her that this is her time to explore and learn and play. Give her the tools and toys she needs to role play the stories of strong women!

2. So that they learn to believe in themselves!

Not for a moment do I want my daughters to ever doubt themselves or think that they can't do something just because they are female. As their mother, they need to see me speaking positively about myself and my abilities.

They also need to see me doing stuff that is hard, so that they know that they can do hard things, too!

3. So that they strive to become powerful leaders in their community!

Make sure your daughters know who the female leaders are both in your local area, as well as worldwide. Strong female role models in leadership are so instrumental in encouraging young women to not be passive followers, but leaders themselves. We want our girls to not be afraid to take charge and be confident in their place in this world.

4. So that they are motivated to pursue STEM careers!

Introduce your daughters to women who have successful careers in Science, Technology, Engineering, and Mathematics. Get your girls talking about their own capabilities and desires for successful careers in fields that otherwise might not seem attainable. Teach them that they have a lot to contribute and that the world is ready for them.

Techbridge Girls in "How Role Models Can Make the Difference for Girls" reminds us that "Many engineers recount that their interest came from early build- or take-apart projects or from the encouragement of a parent who was an engineer. What about girls who haven't been encouraged to tinker or take things apart, or girls who don't know an engineer? This is the reality for many girls. Often girls are simply not exposed to experiences that would encourage their interests in engineering. In fact, messages that they receive from the media or in school or at home tell them that engineering is not for girls."

5. So that they know they have a voice!

Our girls need to be heard. When vocal role models speak up and speak out, our kids are listening. They get to see firsthand what happens when a confident female uses her words to enact change. Let them know that they don't have to be silent or "go along to get along." They must be shown that what they have to say matters!

6. So that they seek a future of independence and strength!

Women are not powerless creatures who need someone to carry them through life. As a mom, I want my girls to see me handling my business and not relying heavily on someone else to get done what I can do and there is very little that I can't do. This is the future I wish for my daughters so that they never feel helpless or incapable.

7. So that they aspire to greatness!

Women have so much to offer this world. When little girls get a chance to watch other females do great things that matter, it reminds them that they also can do awesome things. Whether these great things are big or small doesn't really matter, but it is so encouraging to watch our children catch the vision to make a difference in someone else's life.

8. So that they will be inspired to work towards their dreams!

What does your daughter dream of becoming? Find a mentoring female role model that will help her pursue her passion and get them together! If you don't know anyone personally, then help her find stories of women who have successfully realized their dreams so that she can feel the power of accomplishment and seek to do the same.

9. So that they in turn will become strong female role models!

One good turn deserves another. Let's continue the cycle! When we get our girls inspired and they become successful, it is inevitable that some other little girls in the future will want to emulate them. And when we start this ball rolling, may it never stop! When your daughter knows why girls need strong female role models then she will want to be one, too!

10. So that they can be world changers!

May our daughters see what women can do and then BE the change they want to see in the world. Successful role models give our little girls a brighter future and hope for tomorrow. Each generation gets a new chance to make a difference, whether through innovation, courageousness, kindness, inspiration, or navigating conflict.

Together, women and girls can make a difference!

Importance Of Girl Child Education In Our Society

by Ajay singh | Posted on April 3, 2021

Educating the girl child leads to every perspective of education that strives at improving the skill and experience of girls. This comprises the general education at schools, colleges, professional education, vocational education, and technical education, etc. Here know the importance of girl child education in our society. Education is a vital part of a living being, whether it is a boy or a girl. Education assists an individual to be smarter, to learn new things, and to know about the facts across the globe.

Education is regarded to be the grounds of our community because it is one of the quickest and most efficient methods of encouraging economic growth in any nation. It is perceived to be the important key to terminating poverty and crime towards females. Educating the girls of a nation from the best schools in India also promotes children's and women's endurance rates and health issues, child marriage, empowers women both at their workplace and also their home, and assist in dealing with climate change.

An educated girl can educate their entire family. For the improvement of Indian society or the complete world, girls should be well educated. On some days for the development of Indian and India society girls are working better. In every region of development girls' education is most vital. Understanding the significance of women's education, the administration and various non-government organizations took several projects to increase women's education. So now here we will know the significance of girl education.

 The Importance Of Girl Child Education In Our Society:1. Assist In Buildings More Stable Communities

Assist In Buildings More Stable Communities

Education offers strength and versatility which allows the nation to improve at a quicker rate from any dispute. The overall quality education can even assist prevent disputes in the first place by giving knowledge on social skills, problem-solving, and critical thinking at the schools. And when the main education is essential to girls and secondary education can be a transformative perspective in their life.

2. Promote Gender Equality

In today's society, gender equality continues to be a prevalent problem because of the persistent gap in terms of access to chances for women and men. Gender equality is a basic human right that every human being is entitled to regardless of race, sexuality, ethnicity, or religion. The role men and women play in society is completely determined and as a result, there is a gender gap. When girls in our community are more educated, more influence is placed on gender equality.

As women get equality, human rights become a powerful value of societies as women in governance tend to fight for underprivileged groups. Women's leadership in government also becomes more prevalent, and when women lead, women push for more impartial rules of governance.

3. Allow Girls To Make Their Own Decision

Allow Girls To Make Their Own Decision

Educated girls gave higher courage and independence to make decisions that change their lives. They are better promoted to examine the social imperative that women reside in the home, growing children and doing the regular housework. Education from the best schools in India enables young women to think beyond cultural standards and continue their desires for a better life.

4. Strengthens Economies And Advances The Fight To End Poverty

One of the clearest and obvious benefits of educating girl child from the best schools in India is the prospect for the economic development of a country. The similar even affects the country's Gross Domestic Product (GDP) rate with an increase in women education participation. When women of a country are learned and educated, the whole economy develops and flourishes.

5. Positive Change For Future Generations

Positive Change For Future Generations

The educated girl becomes an educated woman. Offering girls with education is a primary step in developing future generations of healthy, educated, and empowering girls. Educated women of the community can become future leaders, direct towards transformation, and build more powerful and significant societies. And therefore a nation is regarded only as wealthy because of its citizens.

6. Choice To Opt A Profession Of Her Choice

It is one of the vital importance of girl child education. The educated girls can demonstrate to be strong in their several professions. When the girl child has the chance to be educated it offers her the better opportunity to become a successful engineer, doctor, or the choice of the profession she wishes.

7. Improved Life And Health

Improved Life And Health

Educating girl child assist in the improvement of a good life. The girl can read and learn about her rights. They won't be trodden down about her rights. There will be a general improvement in their life. Educated girls bring an awareness of the importance and health and hygiene. Through educating girls they can lead a healthy lifestyle.

Girl child education is one of the most vital concepts. Every girl in our society must have to be educated because education is the most influential and vital weapon that can be used to solve the difficulties of human lives

Women with qualities of a good wife are worthy keepers, and they deserve all the care and respect because they have the purest intentions for the home.

What does it mean to be a good wife?

One of the reasons why a woman is tagged a good wife is because of her readiness to make the marriage work. When the couple disagrees, a good wife would follow the lead of her husband and be receptive to resolving issues amicably.

Also, a good wife understands her husband cannot be perfect, so she does not struggle to mold him into her perfect model. Rather, she adjusts to his personality and corrects his shortcomings when he errs.

A good wife displays qualities that not only help build a home and family but also helps her project herself as a good human being.

20 Best qualities of a good wife

More than aiming to be a good wife, it is also essential to have positive attributes as a person, which in turn will reflect in your role as a wife. These qualities will keep all your relationships within the family healthy and balanced.

But if you are unsure what to look for in a good wife specifically, here are 20 qualities of a good wife that will help you in the search better:

1. Caring and compassionate

A good wife exhibits both care and compassion. She is sensitive to the family's needs, and does her best to provide a solution. She understands when her husband is frustrated, and tries to make him happy.

Her caring disposition makes sure the family does not lack in any aspect of life.

2. Sensitive of the little thinA good wife is not oblivious to the little things that happen in the home.

For instance, if the husband does something considered to be small, she does not ignore it. Rather, she warms up lovingly and appreciates him. On the other hand, if the husband is sad about something in the home, she tries her best to fix it.

3. Spends quality time with her husband

Young Couple in Love Sitting in a Autumn Park Leaning Against a Tree Embracing One Another

No matter how busy the good wife's schedule is, she makes time to spend with her husband.

Some women don't spend time with their husbands using excuses like an extremely busy schedule. A good wife understands that the quality time spent maintains the spark in the marriage.

4. Encourages her husband

One important role of a wife in a man's life is acting as a source of encouragement and support.

In both good and bad times, one of the qualities of a good wife is to encourage and show her husband that he is loved. When men experience challenging times, they don't see their value.

5. Respects her husband

A successful marriage thrives on respect. If you are searching for the characteristics of a good wife, make sure she is respectful.

In addition, a good wife appreciates her husband's effort, and the husband reciprocates with respect and love.

Related Reading:

How to Respect Your Spouse

6. Puts her family first

If you are thinking of what to look for in a wife, know that a good wife puts her family first.

The family's needs and wants top her priorities, and she's not apologetic about it. A good wife goes the extra mile to ensure her home is comfortable for her husband and kids.

7. Husband's best friend and lover

A good wife does not cheat because her husband is her one and only lover.

In addition, she could have close friends, but her husband remains her best friend. If there are any pending issues, she talks first to her husband, who doubles as her best friend.

How To Make Your Spouse Your Best Friend

8. A good problem-solver

In marriage, one of the qualities of a good wife to look for is her willingness and ability to tackle problems.

A good wife neither leaves all the problems to her husband to solve nor points accusing fingers at anyone. Instead, she works together with her husband to combat these problems.

9. Treasures teamwork

What makes a good wife is her ability to collaborate and participate as an active team-player. She does not leave her husband to tackle any issue alone.

Rather, she contributes her quota, and she acknowledges her husband's effort. A good wife knows that collaborative efforts keep the marriage intact as everything goes smoothly.

10. Doesn't infringe on her husband's personal space

A good wife understands that everyone needs their personal space.

When she notices her husband needs some alone time, she respects his decision. She is also clairvoyant as she knows the right time to warm up to her husband and cheer him up.

11. She is romantic

Loving Couple Hugging Together Corner In The Room With Hot Air Balloon

When it comes to romance, a good wife knows how to integrate this into her marriage.

She plans surprises and does little things that catch her husband unaware. She is sensitive to her husband's needs, and leverages this to make romantic gestures.

12. She avoids pretense

A good wife is always true to herself and her words. She isn't a copycat.

Although she has mentors and role models, she remains authentic and her true self because that's what matters to her husband and her marriage.

13. Communicates effectively

Being a good wife requires the input of effective communication.

When there are issues in the marriage, she tries to keep an open communication instead of being silent about them. She prevents her husband from guessing as she lays bare her mind and proffers ways to move forward.

14. Brings out the best in her husband

One of the important attributes of a good wife is her ability to ensure her husband attains his best potential.

She provides her husband with the commitment and support he needs to conquer grounds. She knows how powerful her position is in the family, and she uses it to her husband and home's advantage.

15. She gives a listening ear

One of the traits of a good wife is her ability to give a listening ear because she knows it aids effective communication.

Hence, instead of just hearing, she listens to understand her husband. When her husband wants to discuss with her, she keeps all distractions at bay to focus on him.

16. Celebrates her husband's achievement

One of the attributes of a good woman is she doesn't see her husband's achievement as a means to compete. Rather, she appreciates him and acknowledges his efforts.

If there are children, she seizes the opportunity to use her husband's success to motivate them.

17. She is honest

A man can only trust his wife when she has proved to be honest countless times.

Lasting marriages are built on honesty and effective communication. There's a twist to being honest; you don't have to say anything plainly. For instance, if you don't like his shoes, you can replace them by getting new pairs.

How Important Is Integrity in Relationships

18. Creative in bed

Generally, men love women who are good in bed and vice-versa.

In fact, for some men, it is one of the important qualities of a good wife in a relationship. A good woman does research on how to satisfy her husband in bed. So, he doesn't look outside.

19. Her spiritual life is top-notch

A good wife takes her spiritual life seriously because she knows it is beneficial to her husband and home. She prays for her husband and home, and she meditates regularly.

Also, she ensures her husband is doing well spiritually because it helps them bond better in faith.

20. Remains positive for her husband and home

When things are looking bleak in the home, a good wife knows she has to maintain a positive attitude for the atmosphere to remain cool.

In addition to remaining positive, she keeps the home in good shape even when it is frustrating.

Above all, one of the qualities of a good wife is knowing that her home has to be a safe place for the family to grow, play and live.

Hence, she is unrelenting in achieving this. If you are searching for the best wife qualities, the attributes in this article will guide you in making the right decisions.

When you see a woman you like, hold intelligent conversations around these qualities of a good wife to provide an insight into the kind

CHAPTER 11

What Are The Greatest Strengths Of A Woman?

I will be brief, but I really wanted to set this up because there are incredible women doing incredible things. And it's great to have this platform to highlight these amazing women. Every day to me is apart of women's history month because every single day women are breaking down barriers and making history and changing history. However for the month of March I wanted to do something special. So to start off the month I asked many women this question…..

"What Are The Greatest Strengths Of A Woman?"

"The greatest strength that women possess is the ability to persevere when obstacles are presented to us. We have a specific skill set relying partly on our own intuition to make difficult decisions. Worldwide women are still striving for equal rights in their respective countries. Nevertheless women continue to persevere and accept any challenge presented to us."

"I believe that one of the greatest strengths of women are their ability to adapt; allowing them to be both vulnerable and nurturing and strong and independent. Women are often put in the category of being weak, doing household chores and working as secretaries. All roles of which people would describe as a typical role for women. It was not until WWI that people began to know what women are actually capable of. Most men were at war and those roles usually filled by men were now filled by women because they had to adapt and be strong for their family. Today, there are many men who abuse this strength of women, leaving behind single parent households and young lives affected. The hardship only strengthens the woman to further adapt and be the best version of them that they can be. Therefore, I consider the strength of adapting one of the greatest strength that a woman can have."

"A woman's greatest strength is her ability to let nothing and no one remove her crown. Strong winds may blow, but a QUEEN will bobby pin that thang in place and persevere because she is more than a conquer.

Time may be ticking against her womb, but her patience will produce the children she longs for. Advancement may seem like an impossibility working a job she may hate, but she will maintain her integrity and her work ethic until God lays a career path at her feet. Her KING may be getting on her last black nerve, but she will knuck if you buck for her marriage because it is worth fighting for.

Social media may tell her she needs to be 36-24-36, but she will embrace every dimple and curve with 2 scoops of ice cream; she's the cherry on top. QUEENS walk that walk and talk that talk. We say what we mean and mean what we say. OUR yes is "yes" and our no is "no". Family members may critique her choices but a QUEEN will not be swayed.

A woman's strength is her resilience, her conviction to stand firm, come whatever may. A woman is strong because she knows who she is and whose she is. She's kept woman because God is a keeper. Many will be against her, but a strong woman knows God is for her. You can try and test a strong woman, a QUEEN with a crown that be down for whatever, but I wouldn't recommend it."

"What are the greatest strengths of a woman?" A woman is a giver of life. God allows a man to impart to her the essence of life and she cares and develops that life form until birth. His plan is together they would raise a family but sadly so many women have to raise their children alone. I admire a woman who can raise strong children and lay a pattern of success by her example of life. A strong woman is spiritual, graceful, kind, but can assert herself and defend her dignity. She can bond a family and make her husband and community proud of all she achieves"

"The greatest strength of a woman is her resiliency and inner power. Women are strong, women are survivors, and women are warriors. Through working as a stripper and working at a crisis line for sexual assault & domestic violence, I have seen women come out of unimaginable trauma. I have seen women survive rape and abusive relationships and I too am a survivor.

Not only do women find a way to survive, but they find community and joy. I see these women who have experienced so much hurt, cry and laugh and lift each other up. A woman's greatest strength is her deep power within, the strength to keep going, and the ability to find love and laughter in a world that is not always kind."

"It took me some time to process this question. As my first response was to say being born a Black Woman was a given. I can speak only as an expert in this area of thought with lived experience credentials. I chose to then lean into my curiosity and wonder in imagining why a perceived and identified Black Man could ponder such a question to inquire varied opinions from other Black Women. And because I believe in the spirit of inquiry from this blogger asking such a question.

If you know a Black Woman, you already know her strengths, her growing edges, her survival skills to adapt and code switch as needed. Securing the bag, the eggs, and guarding the gates are daily routines of a Black Woman growing her capacity and bending thru some stretchy situations. The strength of a Black Woman to soak in Epsom salt and bath bombs with rose pedals because that's affordable health care.

The strength of a Black Woman to hold down her family, faith, career, and her dreams to see others do well. The strength of a Black Woman who survived sexual abuse and molestation, got up out of some grave situations, and press toward the mark of my high calling as a Black Woman with being Strong is my strength and is all inclusive. And I celebrate the Black Men that lift us up and would rush to flood this narrative of the greatest strengths of Black Women you know. "

"I believe that women were blessed with many strengths. One being our intuition of course having that ability to be able sense when there is something going on or wrong is one of our many super powers. A few others such as compassion and Empathy is also something that sets us apart from the opposite sex. Our greatest strength of them all however is to be able to carry another human being in our body for 9 months and nature them along the way. Women are amazing we are very strong and we take a lot from the world. Some of us are single mothers such as myself who have to tap into our strength of determination and perseverance to make a way for my families.

Overall women have made major contributions to the universe we have many hidden strengths and talents but our best one is unconditional love."

I feel like the strengths of women are varied. I think as women we have a certain resilience about us that we've kind of adapted over time for survival. We have to be strong enough to raise families, to rise against inequality, even fighting societal pressure set for us and breaking those stigmas. And sometimes just for ourselves in order to just make it to another day. But it's that drive and vision within us to get things done that constantly pushes us. Sometimes women are strong by requirement, not always because we want to be, but because we have to protect ourselves. But everyday we break down barriers and doors that were once closed to us.

"With being a woman there comes a lot of factors. Sometimes people may stereotype us as "crazy" or "always having to be right" but honestly what would the world be without us? Not everyone is perfect, but us women do have many strengths that make us stand out. Besides from being sensitive and emotional at times we are strong, independent, motivational individuals. Take a look from our point of view: some of us are mothers and some of us are working and in school for instance. As a mother myself (of twins at that), it has made me a stronger person.

Yes one may say "My children saved me" but what's worth saying it unless it's meaningful? I take care of them 25|8 from doctor's appointments to feeding them to staying up late nights after I've worked a 12 hour shift! It gets hard at times but it's never worth giving up. On the other-hand, if you are in school or working that shows as a woman that you are willing to get out and better yourself.

Those long hours of studying, homework, and working will definitely pay off in the long run! No matter what you're doing as long as you're doing it for the right reasons keep striving. As women as a whole we are powerful beyond mesasures! In closing in my Beyoncé voice *Who run the world? Girls* lol"

"At a time women were not equally accepted. We were overlooked and shadowed upon, but over the course of the years we have proven to be some phenomenal people. Some strengths of a woman that stand out to me are: power and courage. Starting with power as I mentioned before women weren't always treated equally, however we have managed to earn rights such as voting, getting an education, joining the military, and working in the same career fields as men.

Moving along to courage. Courage says a lot about ones self and in my point of view it brings value to a woman's character. Being that if you have a courage you are willing to take risks and do things that are outside of the box regardless of anyone's options or approvals. In closing, my advice to all of you women out there is to always stay true to yourself and never let your crown tilt!"

What are the greatest strengths of a woman?

Obviously, you will get different answers depending on the woman but speaking as a Queen... Royals, let me make it plain.

I always said a woman's greatest strength is her mind. She can outsmart a man, with her mind! She can talk circles around her boss, with her mind! She can teach her childto grow up strong, with her mind! She is allowed the be the proudest woman alive, with her mind!

A woman's physical appearance is temporary but constantly growing one's mind is the sexiest. Yes, a man will tell you your looks is what caught his eyes but it's your mind that will keep him. They may not act like it but men like to be kept engaged. How do you keep a man engaged? Yes, sex is one way.

Another way is intriguing communication. EX: Find a subject you both like... sports, current events, careers, etc. and start up a conversation about it. Keep your mind quick and strong by reading or researching updated material on the subject. Keep your mind innovative and fresh... this trait will always be a woman's greatest strengths!

Every woman is a strong woman. The things we endure and emulate, the struggles but also the successes that we have all shared make us strong. It's impossible for a woman to not be strong. We are born of strength and we walk with it every day. Look around you at your mother's, your sisters, your daughters and tell me you don't see strength? Whether she is silent or outspoken, she is strong.

I hate to generalize or to say that one characteristic belongs to women only, but I admire how so many women make so much out of nothing. How they've created opportunity out of closed doors, how they've broken ceilings and built the lives they want for themselves. When you hear these incredible stories from women in all walks of life, from single mothers working two jobs to give their children a better life, to businesswomen who are passionate to change the world. No matter the women, no matter her circumstance, never count her out, or presume to know what she is capable of.

A women has no limitations, she can do anything she puts her mind to, such is her strength.

The greatest strengths of a woman would be

Resilience: This is the greatest strength of a woman if you ask me. From puberty, she begins to experience periods and PMS. A woman's body undergoes many changes when she begins to give birth. From stretch marks to cellulite to weight gain. Through all these changes, a woman smiles and carries on.

Courage: Another strength of a woman is courage. Being an engineer and working a predominantly male working environment, I have had to tackle issues bordering on sexual harassment and the ideology that the female is weaker, but courage has been one of my forte and I believe women are courageous.

Self Esteem: Every woman needs a high self-esteem, a great self confidence in her herself, in whom she is. After all, the best outfit you can wear as a woman is confidence.

To recap, Resilience. Courage and Self esteem are the greatest strengths of a woman

I think the greatest strength and a woman is her incredible ability to love most women are emotional creatures by nature we feel things very strongly especially when it comes to the people we love when you think about it it seems as if we are biologically created to love a woman has breast so that she can feed her children a womb so that she can house her unborn child that has to be love. So many times you'll hear of person say why does she stay with him? Someone who wasn't good for her and her answer will be because she loves him even if loving him is to her own detriment women have the incredible ability to put people above themselves even if it hurts them.

The greatest strengths of a woman is her ability to love unconditionally and keep her head held high even when her world seems to be falling apart. Too many times we see women who have the broadest smiles you will ever see, but behind that smile is a broken heart. Strength is carrying life for 9 months. Strength is staying up all night with a sick child and still waking up early and going to work and making sure dinner is ready by the time everyone comes home. Strength is still fighting for what you want even though the world says because you are a woman you can't do this.

6 WOMEN'S STRENGTHS THAT YOU SHOULD BE PROUD OF

WOMEN'S STRENGTHS #1: COLLABORATION

Women often request ideas from the entire team and get group buy-in. Women are also great at sharing information and delegating.

WOMEN'S STRENGTHS #2: CALM UNDER PRESSURE:

Women can handle tough situations with a sense of calm without getting aggressive. Women can also appear less threatening by establishing trust quickly with the men they manage.

WOMEN'S STRENGTHS #3: ATTENTION TO DETAIL:

Women are known to be organized and detailed and can usually handle doing a lot of things at once.

WOMEN'S STRENGTHS #4: OPENNESS:

Women can be open and honest and share a lot of information about tasks and results.

WOMEN'S STRENGTHS #5: INTUITION:

From my experience, women can often tap into other people's needs faster and more effectively than men. One of women's strengths is that they can often pick up very subtle clues about how the people around them are feeling.

WOMEN'S STRENGTHS #6: EMPATHY:

Women are often more capable than men of showing concern for other people's feelings and connecting on a personal level.

Before you go any further, take some time to reflect on the above leadership strengths and write down 2 more women's strengths that you have right now. Then, write down two female l7 Health Tips Every Woman Should Take to Heart

Many women fall into the habit of taking care of others' health and wellness needs before they take care of their own.

But the fact is that you're actually in a better position to provide care for the people most important to you when you make your own healthcare a top priority.

No matter what your age or overall health status is, these 7 health tips can help you increase your chances of better health throughout your life:

1.) Stop smoking. Doing so will greatly reduce your chances of developing lung and heart disease.

2.) Stay on top of your annual wellness checks*. This habit can increase the chances of early detection of disease or chronic conditions, which in turn increases your chances of doing something about any health problems you develop.

3.) Don't skimp on sleep. Besides fighting the signs of aging, regular sleep promotes mental alertness and helps keep your stress levels in check.

4.) Avoid the sun during 10 a.m. and 2 p.m. When you do have to be outside, wear a broad-spectrum sunscreen with a SPF of 30 or higher.

5.) See your doctor every year. Even if you are feeling fine, regular wellness checks and health screenings can increase your chances of early detection of problems.

6.) Make physical activity* an important part of your life. Even if you only have time for 20 minutes of exercise a day, a lifelong habit of regular activity benefits your healthy heart and helps you stay on top of your weight and your stress levels.

7.) Make good nutrition a priority. Avoid crash diets or overindulgence in favor of a realistic diet that features plenty of fruits and vegetables.

CHAPTER 12

Women and food they need to eat

Regardless of a woman's age, nutrition experts generally recommend a diet that is focused on fruits, vegetables, fiber and protein. Your physician can direct you to appropriate resources- such as choosemyplate.gov – to help you tailor a diet that best supports lifelong health.

Women of childbearing age also need foods with folic acid (like leafy green vegetables, beans, and citrus fruits) to help prevent birth defects.

For women who have gone through menopause, it's recommended that you increase your intake of foods with calcium and Vitamin D (such as seafood, fruit, low-fat dairy, and egg yolks) in order to prevent bone disease.

MORE ABOUT PHYSICAL ACTIVITY:

Throughout your life, a physical activity regimen that includes 20-30 minutes of daily cardiac activity (such as walking, running, swimming, hiking, or biking) is recommended for heart health, weight management, and stress reduction. Particularly as you get older, it may be beneficial to supplement your exercise routine with weight lifting or other strength training activities that help prevent loss of bone density and muscle mass.

The good news about exercise is that it's never too late to start. Even if you're past 50 and don't have much of a history of physical fitness, you can still "start small" and work your way into a regular routine of exercise that helps you improve your overall health.

Skin Cancer: Women of all ages should develop the habit of paying attention to changes in the skin or changes in moles and birthmarks. Be sure and report anything that seems different when you have annual wellness checks. If you have risk factors for skin cancer, such as a family history, fair skin, or a history of childhood sunburns, you should ask your physician if he or she recommends regular screenings.

Diabetes: Besides knowing the signs and symptoms of diabetes and managing your risk factors, you may need regular screenings from age 40 onward, depending on your family history and risk factors. Ask your physician for advice.

ea balanced eating pattern is a cornerstone of health. Women, like men, should enjoy a variety of healthful foods from all of the foods groups, including whole grains, fruits, vegetables, healthy fats, low-fat or fat-free dairy and lean protein. But women also have special nutrient needs, and, during each stage of a woman's life, these needs change.

Eating Right

Nutrient-rich foods provide energy for women's busy lives and help to reduce the risk of disease. A healthy eating plan regularly includes:

At least three ounce-equivalents of whole grains such as whole-grain bread, whole-wheat cereal flakes, whole-wheat pasta, bulgur, quinoa, brown rice or oats.

Three servings of low-fat or fat-free dairy products including milk, yogurt or cheese; or calcium-fortified soymilk. (Non-dairy sources of calcium for people who do not consume dairy products include calcium-fortified foods and beverages, canned fish and some leafy greens.)

Five to 5-and-a-half ounce-equivalents of protein foods such as lean meat, poultry, seafood, eggs, beans, lentils, tofu, nuts and seeds.

One-and-a-half to two cups of fruits — fresh, frozen, canned or dried without added sugars.

Two to two-and-a-half cups of colorful vegetables — fresh, frozen or canned without added salt

Iron-rich Foods

Iron is important to good health, but the amount needed is different depending on a woman's stage of life. For example, iron needs are higher during pregnancy and lower after reaching menopause. Foods that provide iron include red meat, chicken, turkey, pork, fish, kale, spinach, beans, lentils and some fortified ready-to-eat cereals. Plant-based sources of iron are more easily absorbed by your body when eaten with vitamin C-rich foods. To get both these nutrients at the same meal, try fortified cereal with strawberries on top, spinach salad with mandarin orange slices or add tomatoes to lentil soup.

Folate (and Folic Acid) During the Reproductive Years

When women reach childbearing age folate (or folic acid) plays an important role in decreasing the risk of birth defects. The requirement for women who are not pregnant is 400 micrograms (mcg) per day. Including adequate amounts of foods that naturally contain folate, such as oranges, leafy green vegetables, beans and peas, will help increase your intake of this B vitamin. There also are many foods that are fortified with folic acid, such as breakfast cereals, some rice and breads. Eating a variety of foods is recommended to help meet nutrient needs, but a dietary supplement with folic acid also may be necessary. This is especially true for women who are pregnant or breastfeeding, since their daily need for folate is higher, 600 mcg and 500 mcg per day, respectively. Be sure to check with your physician or a registered dietitian nutritionist before starting any new supplements.

Daily Calcium and Vitamin D Requirements

For healthy bones and teeth, women need to eat a variety of calcium-rich foods every day. Calcium keeps bones strong and helps to reduce the risk for osteoporosis, a bone disease in which the bones become weak and break easily. Some calcium-rich foods include low-fat or fat-free milk, yogurt and cheese, sardines, tofu (if made with calcium sulfate), tempeh, bok choy, soy beans, sesame seeds, green leafy vegetables and calcium-fortified foods and beverages, such as plant-based milk alternatives, juices and cereals. Adequate amounts of vitamin D also are important, and the need for both calcium and vitamin D increases as women get older. Good sources of vitamin D include fatty fish, such as salmon, eggs and fortified foods and beverages, like milk, as well as some plant-based milk alternatives, yogurts and juices.

Women should be mindful of sources of added sugars, saturated fat and alcohol.

The 2020-2025 Dietary Guidelines for Americans recommend limiting added sugars to less than 10% of daily calories. Limit added sugars including, sugar sweetened beverages, candy, cookies, pastries and other desserts.

The 2020-2025 Dietary Guidelines for Americans specify that on days when alcohol is consumed, women of legal age who choose to drink (and it is not contraindicated, such as during pregnancy) should limit consumption to one drink or less per day. One drink is equal to 12 ounces of beer, 5 ounces of wine or 1.5 ounces of liquor. Women who are pregnant should avoid consuming alcohol altogether.

Focus on sources of unsaturated fats, such as vegetable oils, nuts and seeds, in place of foods high in saturated fat. Opt for low-fat or fat-free dairy products and lean proteins instead of their full-fat counterparts.

Balancing Calories with Activity

Since women typically have less muscle, more body fat and are smaller than men, they need fewer calories to maintain a healthy body weight and activity level.

Women who are more physically active may require more calories.

Physical activity is an important part of a woman's health. Regular physical activity helps with muscle strength, balance, flexibility and stress management.ership strengths that you want to imWhat is healthy eating?

Healthy eating is a way of eating that improves your health and helps prevent disease. It means choosing different types of healthy food from all of the food groups (fruits, vegetables, grains, dairy, and proteins), most of the time, in the correct amounts for you. Healthy eating also means not eating a lot of foods with added sugar, sodium (salt), and saturated and trans fats.

Healthy eating also means getting nutrients primarily from food rather than from vitamins or other supplements. Some women might need vitamins, minerals, or other supplements at certain times in life like before or during pregnancy. But most women, most of the time, should get their essential nutrients from what they eat and drink.

What you eat and drink is influenced by where you live, the types of foods available in your community and in your budget, your culture and background, and your personal preferences. Often, healthy eating is affected by things that are not directly under your control, like how close the grocery store is to your house or job. Focusing on the choices you can control will content. These powerful anti-inflammatory fatty acids can help decrease your odds of dying from heart disease by more than 33 percent, help lower your risk of arthritis, and possibly make your baby smarter. To see which omega-3 fish you should be reeling in, check out our exclusive report of fish ranked for nutritional benefits.

2   Dark Chocolate

dark chocolate

Shutterstock

Attention, chocoholics! Dozens of studies show that people who consume cocoa—as a hot drink or as dark chocolate—are in much better cardiovascular shape than those who don't. One nine-year study in the journal Circulation Heart Failure found women who ate one to two servings of high-quality chocolate per week had a 32 percent lower risk of developing heart failure than those who said no to the cocoa. Researchers attribute cocoa's health benefits to its high concentrations of polyphenols and flavanols, anti-inflammatory compounds that help protect the heart. When you're buying it, just make sure to pick up dark chocolate that contains 74 percent or more cocoa solids, as these are the flavanol-rich compounds.

3   Walnuts

Food for women walnuts

Shutterstock

One in four American women die of heart disease every year and 90 percent of women have one or more risk factors for developing cardiovascular disease. Protecting your most vital organ is as simple as adding some walnuts to your diet. This heart-shaped nut is teeming with antioxidants and omega-3 fatty acids that can help keep you safe. One recent study found that munching on two ounces a day could significantly improve blood flow to and from the heart in just 8 weeks. Another study found that the same amount can help delay development of breast cancer and slow tumor growth in mice. Speculation is that antioxidants called phytosterols, already known cancer fighters, could be the culprit.

4   Sprouted Garlic

Food for women garlic

Shutterstock

Nearly a third of women between 45 and 55 have high blood pressure, an illness that can lead to more serious issues like heart disease or stroke, and that number increases from 50 to 70 percent for women aged 55 to those 65 and older. It turns out, the vampire-repelling plant is both a flavor essential and a heart-disease-fighting superstar. Garlic contains phytochemicals, including allicin, which a review in the Journal of Integrated Blood Pressure Control showed may decrease high blood pressure by as much as 10 points—similar to standard blood pressure medication. Garlic can also prevent the progression of heart disease by reducing the accumulation of plaque and preventing the formation of new plaque in the arteries, according to a study in the Journal of Nutrition. The catch is that cooking destroys this beneficial compound, so you'll have to use garlic powder, aged garlic extract, or sprouted garlic.

5   Olive Oil

Food for women olive oil

Shutterstock

A study in the New England Journal of Medicine found that the Mediterranean diet, which includes healthy fats like olive oil, prevents about 30 percent of heart attacks, strokes and deaths from heart disease in people at high cardiovascular risk. Olive oil, in particular, is loaded with monounsaturated fats (MUFAs), which lower "bad" LDL cholesterol and raise "good" HDL cholesterol, which helps in lowering your risk of heart disease.

6   Apples

Food for women apples

Shutterstock

One of the best foods women should be eating is one you probably already are: the apple. Metabolic syndrome—a syndrome that refers to a cluster of conditions like insulin resistance, high blood pressure, and high cholesterol—is the main contributor to heart disease, the leading killer of American women. While women who eat a diet rich in blood-sugar-spiking refined carbs or those who are overweight are most susceptible to metabolic syndrome, even healthy postmenopausal women are also at risk. The Iowa Women's Health Study, which has been tracking 34,000 women for nearly 20 years, found that apples are one of three foods most effective at reducing the risk of death from coronary heart disease and cardiovascular disease among women, as these women had less abdominal fat and lower blood pressure than their peers who didn't consume apples.

7   Oatmeal

Food for women oatmeal

Shutterstock

High cholesterol can lead to the buildup of plaque in artery walls. Left untreated, this buildup can lead to heart attack and stroke, resulting in 2 of the top 5 leading causes of death in American women. Luckily, it's not too difficult to combat. Simply eating a healthy diet that includes soluble fiber-rich whole grains, like oatmeal, can help. Oatmeal can also protect you from heart disease. A Harvard study of more than68,000 women found that those who ate the most fiber daily were 23 percent less likely to develop heart disease than were those who consumed the least. Thanks to the breakfast staple's high fiber content, it can also slash the odds of developing type 2 diabetes by a whopping 61 percent! The superstar nutrient also helps stabilize blood sugar, which wards off diet-derailing hunger and dangerous dips in glucose.

8   Beans

Food for women beans

Shutterstock

Unlike animal sources of protein, beans are free of unhealthy fats. That might be the very reason one study found that people who consumed legumes at least four times a week had a 22 percent lower risk of heart disease compared with those who consumed them less than once a week. Equally as encouraging results were published in the Canadian Medical Association Journal. A scientific review of 26 clinical trials discovered that eating a 3/4 of a cup of beans daily could reduce levels of "bad" cholesterol in the blood by 5 percent.

Foods That Boost Your Brainpower

Shutterstock

According to the Alzheimer's Association, Alzheimer's disease—a neurodegenerative disorder that is the most common type of dementia—is currently the fifth leading cause of death in females, and disproportionately affects women more than men. In fact, almost two-thirds of Americans with Alzheimer's are women, but many experts attribute the disparity to the fact that women often live longer than men, and old age is the greatest risk factor for Alzheimer's. Experts suspect other risk factors to be related to the decrease in consumption of antioxidant-rich foods, which typically scavenge cell-damaging free radicals which may lead to cognitive decline. Fit these foods into your diet to boost your brainpower and nourish your noggin for a longer, more productive life, and then check out which you should avoid.

9   Shrimp

Food for women shrimp

Shutterstock

Shrimp is the most potent source of an essential and hard-to-get nutrient called choline. This neurotransmitter building block is necessary for the structure and function of all cells, and a deficiency in this compound has been linked to neurological disorders and decreased cognitive function. Not only does it act as brain food, but it can also help lower your risk of breast cancer.

10   Cinnamon

Food for women cinnamonhelp you make small changes in your daily life to eat healthierprove on.

Here are the facts about depression in women: In the U.S., about 15 million people have depression each year. Most of them are women. Unfortunately, nearly two-thirds do not get the help they need.

What Is Depression?

Clinical depression is a serious and pervasive mood disorder. It causes feelings of sadness, hopelessness, helplessness, and worthlessness. Depression can be mild to moderate with symptoms of apathy, little appetite, difficulty sleeping, low self-esteem, and low-grade fatigue. Or it can be more severe.

Depression in women is very common. In fact, women are twice as likely to develop clinical depression as men. Up to 1 in 4 women are likely to have an episode of major depression at some point in life

What Are the Symptoms of Depression in Women?Symptoms of depression in women include:

Persistent sad, anxious, or "empty" mood

Loss of interest or pleasure in activities, including sexRestlessness, crankiness, or excessive crying

Feelings of guilt, worthlessness, helplessness, hopelessness, pessimism

Sleeping too much or too little, early-morning waking

Appetite and/or weight loss, or overeating and weight gain

Less energy, fatigue, feeling "slowed down"

Thoughts of death or suicide, or suicide attempts

Trouble concentrating, remembering, or making decisions

Persistent physical symptoms that do not respond to treatment, such as headaches, digestive disorders, and chronic pain

Women and self worth

1. Know Yourself

Building self-esteem first involves knowing who you are: identifying what you like, knowing what you want out of life, and developing an awareness of how your past experiences have shaped the person you are today. It requires paying attention to how you treat yourself and developing an awareness of the internal messages you grapple with.

2. Care for Yourself

Developing healthy self-esteem also encompasses recognizing how powerful your internal voice is and learning to rewire your brain by developing more effective thinking patterns. It involves acting as your own cheerleader and being mindful that things such as diet, exercise, sleep, and setting realistic expectations all play a role in how you feel about yourself. Beyond the basics, caring for yourself means ensuring you take time out to nurture your spirit by doing things you enjoy.

3. Respect Yourself

Respecting yourself is vital to maintaining healthy self-esteem. It involves assessing and upholding your values without sacrificing your well-being to please others. It's about developing trust in yourself and learning skills to become more assertive.

4. Accept Yourself

Fostering healthy self-esteem involves acknowledging your limits and imperfections, accepting mistakes, and learning to more effectively deal with criticisms. It necessitates knowing your threshold for stress, developing self-compassion, and forgiving yourself for faults or missteps.

5. Love Yourself

To truly demonstrate self-esteem, you must believe in your worth and care about your future. Loving yourself means treating yourself as well as you treat friends and loved ones. Doing this involves creating better boundaries in relationships. It also entails celebrating your strengths and learning to accept compliments.

WHY A WOMAN NEEDS TO BE FINANCIALLY INDEPENDENT

Why a Woman Needs To Be Financially Independent

A financially independent woman can support her family in every way possible.

A financially independent woman can support her family in every way possible.

If the woman of a house is self-confident, she can make better decisions for her family.

Financial independence gives you the choice to lead the life of your choice or the way you want to. Women in India face so many hurdles on their way to financial independence. Many don't get the opportunities to achieve; the ones who achieve financial independence at some point have to sacrifice their careers for family or to raise their children.

In these changing times and rising inflation, every member of the family needs to be financially independent. So many women, especially in India, sacrifice their careers once they get married. Most of these women are educated and capable of earning well. However, due to the pressure from their families and society, they leave their jobsafter marriage or after becoming a mother. Here's why women of the family should be financially independent.

Spending capacity of the family:

A financially independent woman can support her family in every way possible. With steep inflation, it is virtually impossible to lead a good life with only one person earning.

Self-Respect

The self-respect of women is often ignored. When a woman is earning, she doesn't need to ask her husband for money for her expenses.

Command respect from the family members

Financially independent women command respect from every member of the family. Women, who are financially dependent on their families, often face disrespect. Even the relatives and neighbours respect a financially independent woman.

Women who are not financially independent, are not able to stand up for themselves or any other oppressed person in society. The husband or other family members may exploit the financial dependence of women to commit atrocities on them.

Increased Self Confidence

Financial Independence provides self-confidence. If the woman of a house is self-confident, she can make better decisions

Conclusions

You all will agree with me in recent past women have been deprived of their rights to speak,they have be denied access to good education,they been robbed of their integrity. In time past women education are known to end in the kitchen thereby making them think less of themselves and been less productive. You will all agree with me on this once one woman is empowered the whole world is,once one woman is made the whole world is because she tends to touch so many life as a mother. Women are nations builder's,they are home makers,give them right sense of direction and see them build the world with lots of love

But the modern girl child needs to be empowered in other to stand up for themselves,need to be taught to defend herself in a good way,need to learn hw to speak out and guide her words carefully. There for I employ our mother to pay more attention to their girl child. Like the saying goes women are wealth and needs to be handled with outmost care and compassion .